The
Bar Mitzvah
Boys

Myron Uhlberg

illustrated by Carolyn Arcabascio

Albert Whitman & Company
Chicago, Illinois

He was an old man, now, with only one regret. Seventy years ago, when he turned twelve, he was unable to begin the traditional yearlong training for his bar mitzvah, the Jewish coming-of-age ceremony that celebrates a boy becoming a man when he is thirteen.

It was a time of war and, along with all the other Jews in his small village in Poland, the Nazis sent him to a concentration camp.

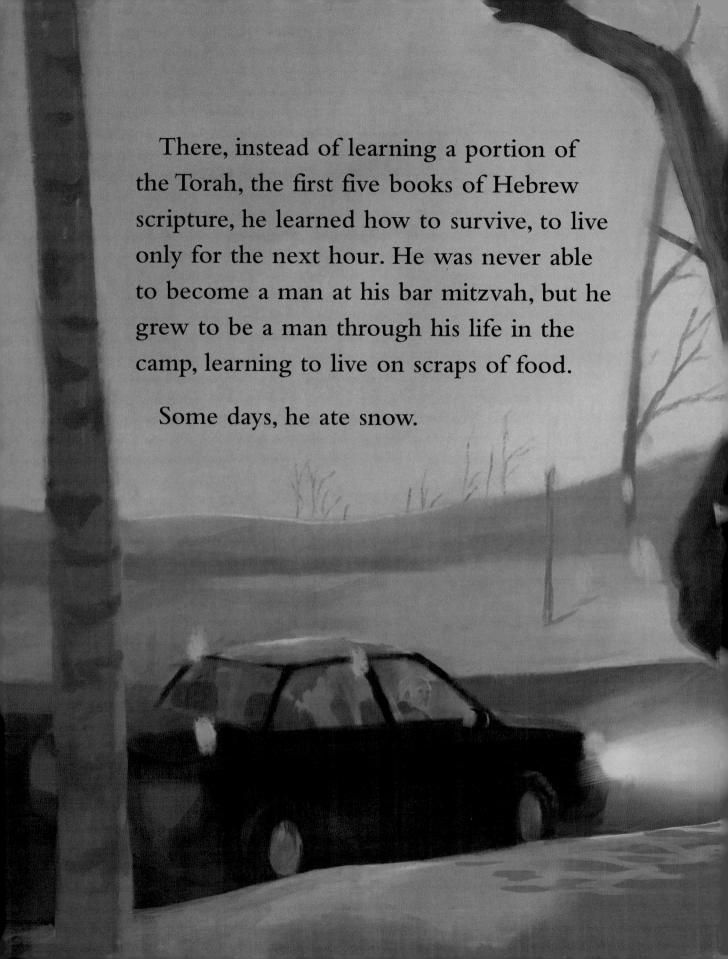

There, instead of learning a portion of the Torah, the first five books of Hebrew scripture, he learned how to survive, to live only for the next hour. He was never able to become a man at his bar mitzvah, but he grew to be a man through his life in the camp, learning to live on scraps of food.

Some days, he ate snow.

And then one day, in
seemingly endless days,
he was free.

The man's grandson didn't think him old. He hardly noticed his grandfather's wrinkles, his spotted hands, and thin hair. He noticed his grandfather's brilliant blue eyes; eyes that saw and understood.

The boy loved his grandfather.

And his grandfather loved him back without measure.

The boy's father felt their love for each other. It made him feel like a link in a chain, a long chain that had been broken because his father had not been bar mitzvahed. So he suggested that his father and his son be bar mitzvahed together.

The boy, so loving his grandfather, said yes.

The grandfather, returning that love, said of course.

For a year, the man and the boy studied together.

They spent hours memorizing the sacred Jewish text, and then they learned how to recite and sing it in Hebrew, the ancient language of their ancestors.

When the man grew tired, the boy held his hand; when the boy grew bored, his grandfather rubbed his neck. And together, they were increasingly absorbed in the ageless ritual of the Jewish people.

This is what I wanted to do when I was twelve, the man thought. I could imagine the joy and pride that would light up my father's face as I prayed, he remembered.

Months passed in a hazy blur of dust motes dancing through streaks of sunlight in the late afternoon shadows of the empty synagogue, while the man and the boy chanted their chosen Torah portions, under the watchful eyes of their teacher, the rabbi, and of the boy's father.

The rabbi had never had such an old student, or as odd a pair of students as the man and the boy. She marveled at their agelessness as they started and completed each passage of the Torah in their increasingly fluent Hebrew.

Together, they bent over the sacred scrolls, their heads touching.

The rabbi saw the years fall from the man's shoulders, seeming to softly land on the boy's bent head. The old man seemed to grow younger, while the boy grew older.

One day, the man and the boy completed their Torah studies. They were ready to be bar mitzvahed.

A day was chosen. It was to be the
day the boy turned thirteen, and the man
achieved the age of eighty-three. They were
born on the same day, a lifetime of years
apart. Together they would celebrate a day
combining remembrance of the past and the
unfolding of the future, recognition of the
unbroken chain.

The chain included the grandfather's father, who was directed by the guard in the camp with the shiny black boots to join the line on the left, and who then directed the boy to the line on the right.

Right or left.

The man, who was
then a boy, never saw
his father again.

Now the old man stood with
his grandson at the altar, eyes glued
to the open Torah, and he felt the
ghostly shadow of his father next to
him; along with the boy's father,
they made four links of the
human chain.

A guitar played, a drum kept time, and the
temple was filled with clapping and singing.

A solemnity filled the temple, borne upward on the old man's memories of the past and the promise of the boy's future.

And they danced to the music,
the old man and the boy.

The boys were
now men.

For my dearest of dear friends,
Sam and Eva Beller.
With a special thanks to Sam, whose
bar mitzvah at eighty-three years of age
was the inspiration for this story
—MU

For Brett
—CA

Library of Congress Cataloging-in-Publication
data is on file with the publisher.

Text copyright © 2019 by Myron Uhlberg
Illustrations copyright © 2019 by Carolyn Arcabascio
First published in the United States of America in 2019
by Albert Whitman & Company
ISBN 978-0-8075-0570-0 (hardcover)
ISBN 978-0-8075-0569-4 (ebook)

Printed in China
10 9 8 7 6 5 4 3 2 1 WKT 24 23 22 21 20 19
Design by Nina Simoneaux

For more information about Albert Whitman & Company,
visit our website at www.albertwhitman.com.

100 Years of Albert Whitman & Company
Celebrate with us in 2019!